MORENO VALLEY
APR 3 0 2001

D0633812

When
Night Comes

When Night Comes

Ron Hirschi

Photographs by Thomas D. Mangelsen

Moreno Valley Public Library

Text copyright © 2000 by Ron Hirschi
Photographs copyright © 2000 by Thomas D. Mangelsen
All rights reserved

Published by Caroline House
Boyds Mills Press, Inc.
A Highlights Company
815 Church Street
Honesdale, Pennsylvania 18431
Printed in Hong Kong

Publisher Cataloging-in-Publication Data

Hirschi, Ron.
When night comes / by Ron Hirschi ; photographs by
Thomas D. Mangelsen. 1st ed.
[32]p. : col. ill. ;   cm.
Summary: A look into the world of animals who come out after sunset.
ISBN 1-56397-766-4
1. Animals—Juvenile literature. 2. Nocturnal animals—Juvenile
literature. [1. Animals.   2. Nocturnal animals.]
I. Mangelsen, Thomas D., ill. II. Title.
591.5—dc21   2000   AC   CIP
98-88219

First edition, 2000
Book designed by Randall F. Llewellyn
The text of this book is set in Goudy

10 9 8 7 6 5 4 3 2 1

Photographs:
Jacket: grizzly bear
Back cover: eagle
Endpapers: sunset

For the kids of
Wakeman and Hartland.
RH

For Helen Gromme, who saw nature
with the innocence of a child.
TM

Night is a hush of twinkling stars,
a cool wind tossing the tips of
trees, and a time for us to sleep
until morning wakes the world.

Outside, beyond our safe, warm houses, darkness falls slowly. In the moments before becoming dark, the night gets ready as creatures of the day trade places with creatures of the night – all who hunt by the moon's pale light.

Sandhill cranes settled for the night

Sandhill cranes at sunset

When blue sky
vanishes, waterbirds
flock together,
dropping like the sun
from the glowing
nighttime sky.

Spotted owls

Without daylight and bright colors to guide them, night hunters listen for the sounds of tiny footsteps.

Owls poke their heads from daytime roosts, then fly to hunt mice that scurry through crunching leaves.

Spotted owl hunting

Coyote

Coyotes hear mice
too, even beneath
a blanket of snow.

They also catch
rabbits sneaking from
daytime burrows.

Desert cottontail

Wolves use sharp eyes and sense of smell to catch a meal before darkness falls. They might even find their biggest prey now, as the air grows cooler and insects are whisked away by evening breezes. Deer and elk can feed in the meadows, where mosquitoes might have kept them away by day.

Gray wolf

Elk at sunset

Moose at sunset

Elk and moose must beware of the wolf. They must keep ears alert for hungry grizzly bears, too. Nightfall is grizzly's moment and the great bear's tracks lead to river, meadow, and deep forests.

Grizzly bear

Grizzlies might go fishing, or stalk newborn calves and fawns, as night shadows begin to darken their mountain homes.

Elk with calf

Marten

The time when shadows fall is also a favorite time for martens, raccoons, and otters. The marten pops from behind a rock, then sneaks along a fallen log. The marten can climb to where squirrels and birds search for safe places to sleep.

River otters

Raccoon

Frog

Otters and raccoons
catch frogs, salamanders,
or baby ducks along the
edge of a pond.

River otter

By day the river otter hunts by sight.
Now it uses sensitive paws and
whiskers to feel for crayfish, a favorite
otter dinner. Mother otters also stand
to sniff the air, trying to keep track of
their playful little ones with their super
sense of smell.

Dark as the night about to come, black bears roam evening woods looking for berries, ants, and tender green grass to fill hungry bear bellies.

Black bear

Beaver

But no one is as busy
in the darkening world
as the beavers –

building new ponds,
repairing their dams, or
adding sticks to a lodge.

Beaver lodge

Beaver splash

After a day hidden away, the beavers gnaw soft white wood of aspen trees, felling tree after tree, well into the night. But if you come too close, beaver splashes with its tail, disappearing from sight.

When all is quiet, a
wood duck might swim
on beaver's pond.

Wood duck

Red fox

Nearby, a baby fox is about to slip into its den, while badger begins a nighttime prowl.

Badger

High above the cooling evening earth, bald eagles fly from their daytime hunting grounds.

Bald eagle

Circling, they gather
together when they
find tall trees just right—
just right to spend this
coming night.

Bald eagles

Afterword

Nightfall is a time when we are safe and comfortable in our houses. But for many animals, this is a very threatening time – dark brings predators out to take advantage of the low light. Predators' sharp eyes, acute hearing, and sense of smell help them catch their prey.

Complete darkness is a time of activity, too, but the moments just before dark are far busier. Animals of the day are still feeding and moving to their night roosts or sleeping places. Insects are cooled by the night air, becoming more available to all who eat them, as their bodies slow down and wingbeats are not as swift and strong.

This is a good time to watch wildlife. Bears, wolves, and other large predators can be seen now, stalking deer, elk, and moose. Owls begin to fly out from tree cover.

Some of the most spectacular nightfall sights include the gathering of eagles. Bald eagles will often fly together in large flocks, seeking safe, communal roosting places in tall trees. This behavior is most often seen in wintertime near major feeding areas such as the salmon streams of the West.

Wherever you live, spend some time listening for the gathering sounds of darkness. It is a special time, much like the break of the new day to come.